Answer The Question

AMY LAURENS

OTHER WORKS

SANCTUARY SERIES

Where Shadows Rise
Through Roads Between
When Worlds Collide

KADITEOS SERIES

How Not To Acquire A Castle
How Not To Ring The Hero's Bell (2019)
How Not To Take Over The World (2019)

SHORT STORY COLLECTIONS

Of Sea Foam and Blood
Darkness and Good

NON-FICTION

How To Write Dogs
How To Theme
How To Create Cultures

Find other works by the author at
www.amylaurens.com

Answer The Question

INKLET #10

AMY LAURENS

Inkprint PRESS

www.inkprintpress.com

Print ISBN: 978-1-925825-09-1
eBook ISBN: 9781386327837

www.inkprintpress.com

*National Library of Australia Cataloguing-in-Publication
Data*
Laurens, Amy 1985 –
Answer The Question
62 p.
ISBN: 978-1-925825-09-1
Inkprint Press, Canberra, Australia
1. Romance—Fantasy 2. Fiction—Short Stories 3.
Romance—Paranormal—General

First Print Edition: May 2019
Cover design © Inkprint Press
Interior art © Amy Laurens

ANSWER THE QUESTION

I TILTED MY HEAD BACK AGAINST THE pastel green wall of the day spa, relaxing just enough that I could feel every ache and pain in my body. Man, I was looking forward to this massage.

The door handle on one of the client rooms twisted, and a fraction of a second before the door opened, I stiffened. Heat sang through my body and, furious, I stuffed it away. Not Brandr. For a brief moment I panicked, wondering if Bianca had mixed things up and booked my massage with him again—but I forced myself to breathe and relax, keeping my eyes closed. Bianca ran her day spa with a golden heart and an iron fist; she wouldn't do that to me.

Still, as Brandr exited the client room and crossed the waiting area, footsteps soft on the rugged floor, I felt more than heard him pause in front of me, every sense in my body standing to rigid attention.

Steady breath in, steady breath out. Steady breath in, steady breath out. I'd managed to successfully ignore him through all of our infrequent encounters since that first massage, and today would be no different.

In front of me, he sniffed. "I clearly need to have a word with Bianca," he muttered, and I couldn't tell if he was including me in his audience or not. "That lounge needs replacing, and some things around here are getting downright old and worn."

I managed to avoid choking on my disbelief until he left the room, though I could still see the back of his head disappearing down the stairs, so doubtless he heard me. Whatever. I didn't even care. Stupid, arrogant, jerk-faced *twat*. Just because he was so pretty that girls fell over themselves to be near him. Well, I wasn't falling for it, even if it *had* been the best bloody massage of my life. I was not some stupid, vapid piece of arm-candy for him to play with. Urgh.

I slammed my head back against the wall just a little too hard, and winced. *Moron. Imbecile! Arrogant peacocky slime-ball!*

"Ellie?" Bianca's soothing voice halted my litany and I sighed, forcing away the frustration that encounters with Brandr always left me. "Your turn, honey."

Damn him. I was going to enjoy my massage. He was not going to ruin this perfect moment of relaxation.

Firmly shoving thoughts of stunningly gorgeous manwhores from mind, I followed Bianca into a treatment room.

<hr>

I slid into my regular seat at Felici's just as Nana and Tanya, my older sister, were handing their menus to the waitress. "I'll have the usual," I said as the waitress raised an eyebrow at me.

She nodded and swept away, leaving behind a cobalt blue bottle that sparkled and dripped with condensation.

"So," I said, pouring water for everyone, "what's new?"

Tanya shrugged. "Nothing much. Working retail during the holiday season still sucks. Though at least Brandr is on this afternoon, so things won't be deadly boring until he finishes up at six."

The glass I reached for slipped, tipped, and sailed towards the floor. Nana, with characteristic lightning reflexes, caught it before it had barely left the table, setting it upright and relieving me of my water-pouring duties.

"Brandr works at the boutique as well?" I said, aiming for nonchalant.

Nana smirked, and I pointedly ignored her.

Sister nodded. "Oh, yeah. He does mornings in the spa and afternoons downstairs in the storefront."

I made a careful mental note to avoid Schwab in the afternoons. Not that I needed much help with that; Schwab was a designer boutique selling jewellery and cosmetics that were at least four times out of my price range.

I'd known they were affiliated with the day spa, but I hadn't realised they shared staff. I guess it made sense, especially for the cosmetics and beauty product sales.

Whatever. Irrelevant.

I shoved the whole issue aside and turned to Nana. "So, I was thinking of hitting up the department store this afternoon. I need some clothes for work. Do you want to come?"

Not only did Nana have impeccable taste, she also had an almost-bottomless bank account, and she had no qualms about sharing it with her two surviving family members.

She nodded decisively. "Yes," she said. "It will be illuminating."

My eyebrows knitted in puzzlement, but I let it pass. Nana was well known for her bizarre comments and apparently unconnected observations. "Sure," I said. "Thank you."

"Swing by Schwab when you're done," Tanya said, setting her empty glass back on the table. "I'm stuck there till eleven tonight. I'll take my break when you come."

Nana was already agreeing enthusiastically, and I groaned. So much for avoiding the place.

Never mind. We'd go in, find Tanya, and drag her out for a break. The chances of running into Brandr were entirely minimal. Everything would be fine.

"I'll just be a second," I assured Nana as I ducked into the shopping centre bathroom.

We'd spent a good couple of hours clothes-hunting, and all of the resulting outfits were nicer than what I had on now. If we were only stopping past Schwab to collect Tanya, my chances of running into Brandr were minimal (thank heavens), but if we did I wasn't interested in providing more fodder for insults. Old and tired. Prat.

Locked safely in a stall, I surveyed my options. The navy was too formal; the silver too attention-seeking. I settled on a neutral-toned skirt that showed off my butt and a red silk blouse with fluttery cap sleeves that managed to actually make me look like I had cleavage. The whole outfit was chic yet effortless, the neutral skirt enriching the light brown of my hair and the red blouse the best possible colour for my skin tone.

I pulled it all on, slipped on some gorgeous new heels—it was so shallow of me, but I did love Nana's bank account—fluffed my hair, and headed back out.

Nana whistled. "Don't you look special," she said.

I smiled distractedly, running my fingers along the blouse's neckline.

"It's missing something," I said. "I need something around my neck."

Nana shrugged. "If you say so."

I loaded my bags back into the trolley and marched off determinedly. Three times Nana tried to draw my attention to jewellery stores we passed, but I knew exactly the one I was after.

We rounded the corner: Schwab. Narrowing my eyes, I made a beeline for the main jewellery display in the back of the store.

Nana caught up after a few moments, and eyed the dazzling array of entirely over-the-top necklaces, the lightest of which looking like it had to weigh at least a pound. "These aren't really what you're looking for, dear," she observed candidly.

I shrugged, stifling irritation. "I thought they'd have a bigger range. This one's okay," I added, pointing out a silver filigreed piece with a floral motif.

Voices erupted around the end of the aisle and I froze. *I will not turn around. I will not turn around.* I realised I was checking myself out in the mirror to make sure the outfit was sitting right, and jerked my gaze away. "Or this one." I reached for another necklace to my left, conveniently allowing me to turn my back on the approaching Prince of Twathood.

Nana, of course, turned towards him. "Oh, *I* see. Of course."

Was it permissible to hit grandmothers for being smug? If it had been Tanya, I'd have whacked her for sure.

"I'll just wait out the front, I think," Nana continued, oblivious to my glares. "My feet, you know. And my hips. And my back." She hobbled away to the tables out the front, looking every day of her age—which I'd never seen her do when she wasn't up to mischief.

I was too busy fuming at her retreating back to realise that Brandr had come within range.

"Can I help you?" he said, eyes dancing.

No. I was *not* looking at his stupid pretty eyeballs. I whirled back to the jewellery display. "That one," I said primly. "I'd like to try it on please."

He reached for the necklace that hung just out of my reach, brushing past my shoulder in the process.

I jolted at the energy his touch sent through me and ended up three feet away down the aisle. My stupid reflexes were always a little unpredictable, but they seemed worse when he was around. This had been an utterly ridiculous idea. So what if he thought I looked old and tired? Why did I care what he thought?

"Here."

I turned back to him, expecting to see the silver filigree. Instead, he held a ropey, glimmering creation I could have sworn wasn't on the shelves a moment ago. It was a single necklace, but made up of tens or maybe even hundreds of strands; I couldn't quite get a fix on it to figure it out. The threads seemed unnaturally fine and soft, like spider's silk, the beads tiny and delicate as dewdrops.

It glimmered gently in the fluorescent lights of the store, and I stood motionless, transfixed.

"Do you like it?" There was a depth of emotion to Brandr's voice that I'd never heard before, and my heart skipped a beat in response.

"Yes," I breathed, awkwardness and irritation forgotten.

Brandr beamed and my pulse skipped again. Saints, he was beautiful. Too beautiful, like a dangerous snake, but as he moved towards me with the necklace in hand, I was powerless to break the spell.

He reached for me and I turned to face the mirror, my back to him so he could fasten the necklace around my neck. Instead, he laid one end of it across my forehead and directed me to hold it in place while he arranged the rest of the multitude of strands through the back of my hair, half catching it up in a style that seemed at once impossibly complex and incredibly simple.

He fastened the catch on the jewellery just above my left ear and dropped a strand of hair to cover it. I stared at the mirror, lost for words. The necklace—headpiece—whatever it was—had glimmered before, but in my hair it shone. I felt like I was wearing a headdress of moonlight that seemed to pulse gently in time with my breaths.

"Stunning."

I glanced up at Brandr in the mirror, surprised to see his eyes shining wetly. That instant was enough to break the spell though, and I turned. "Let me show Nana," I said. "I mean, let me see what she thinks."

He stepped back, deferential. "Of course."

Out the front of the store I found Tanya engaged in vibrant conversation with Nana, who sat with her back to me. Tanya's eyes widened as she spotted me. She paused mid-sentence. Nana twisted in her chair to see what Tanya had seen—and her hand flew to her mouth.

"Oh," she said as I drew close. "Oh, Elyena. You have it in your hair."

I shrugged, suddenly embarrassed. "Oh, well," I said, tugging on the strands across my forehead. "Brandr thought he'd try something different."

"Brandr did this?" Nana asked. She turned back to her table and busied herself in her copious handbag before I could reply.

Irritated, I snagged the necklace and tugged it down over my face. I shook my hair free from it and twisted it around to hang around my neck. Stupid Brandr and his stupid ideas. What was he playing at, anyway?

"There," I snapped at the table, Tanya already engrossed in a new conversation with Brandr, and Nana still rummaging in her bag. Seriously, would it kill them to focus on me for more than a second? "Now what do we think?"

I twitched the luminous white strands that trailed down my chest, still beautiful, but lacking the glorious allure they'd had in the mirror just before.

Brandr narrowed his eyes critically at me. "The shirt does alluring things to your cleavage, I'll give you that, even if it does emphasise your wide shoulders. I still wish you'd let me trim your hair, your forehead's getting completely lost..." He trailed off under my glare. "No?"

"I *meant* about the *necklace*." My voice was remarkably calm for someone struggling not to commit homicide.

Beside him, Tanya laughed. "I'm sorry. I've been training him for months, and he's still barely housebroken." She turned to him. "Brandr, what's our mantra? Answer the question..."

"Nothing else." He nodded. "Answer the question, nothing else."

They repeated it again together before dissolving into giggles.

I shook my head. "I'll just, uh, go put this back then, shall I?"

"Yes, dear," Nana said. "You can try to do that if you like."

I rolled my eyes at her theatrics and headed for the back of the store. I hunted the display shelf for a place to hang the necklace. Oddly, there didn't seem to be any empty hooks. I ran the necklace through my fingers, glancing down at where it hung limply around my neck. It was pretty—magically so—but it lacked the sparkle, the mysterious something else I'd thought it had when Brandr had first put it on me.

On a whim, I faced the mirror and tugged the necklace back up into my hair, trying to mimic the style Brandr had created. Soft strands fell over my forehead and caught my hair partially up; it wasn't quite how he'd done it, but... I tilted my head at the mirror and my heart skipped a beat.

Hesitantly, I reached up to touch the gossamer strands where they glimmered and glowed like a slipped halo.

Something solid hit me across the backs of my thighs. I flailed wildly for balance and found myself clinging to

Brandr's head, as he pranced wildly around the store with me on his shoulders, shouting, "Answer the question, nothing else! Answer the question, nothing else!"

Oh saints, my stomach's showing. I tugged awkwardly at my shirt, caught between fleeting embarrassment and his wildly infectious enthusiasm.

"But what's the question?" I shouted over the din, too disoriented by suddenly being on his shoulders to think of anything better to say.

He laughed. "The necklace! It works!"

"Um, yay?"

Brandr performed some complicated sort of movement that removed me from his shoulders and ended up with me in his arms. "Yay?" he said, eyes oddly serious in contrast to the frivolity of the situation.

"Well," I said, waving my hands as vaguely as I felt, "It works, right? So yay?" I still had no idea what 'working' entailed, but whatever it was, apparently this was Christmas for Brandr.

He hugged me tightly to him and where our skin touched, fire rippled through me. Saints. I'd forgotten what it felt like to have actual proper skin contact with him, not just accidental brushes I did my best to avoid.

It was like drowning, and it was addictive, and it was probably just my imagination that my necklace halo was glowing like it might go nova and Brandr was holding me, touching me, and my hands were wrapping around the back of his neck and through his hair as the air around us burst with perfect, glorious pleasure.

Skin. I needed his skin.

My stomach flipped as something happened to gravity and I had a brief impression of broken plasterboard and a flash of darkness before Brandr lay me down somewhere soft, and all I cared about was the touch of his skin, because it was beautiful, and perfect, and I nearly sobbed as heat soaked through me, lighting up every fibre of my being and chasing out fear and doubt and darkness—except just *there*, in my head, the seat of logic and rationality. *It* remained unmoved, a cold stone trying to catch my attention in the wave of heat.

"Wait," I gasped. I needed a moment to process this.

He ignored me, hands rubbing at my shoulders just like they had that first time in—

I took in the plush-rugged floor, the pastel green walls, the ivory couches around the perimeter of the room. We were in the day spa. I struggled semi-upright. "Wait! How on earth did we..."

He paused, and I found the gaping hole in the floor. Vague memories of a surge of power, of Brandr springing upwards ten metres or more to the roof—*through* the roof—through the *floor*... I stared at him, wide-eyed, the magma flow of heat suddenly halted. "What are you?"

"Happy," he mumbled against my shoulder.

I whacked him gently on the back of the neck. "Answer the question," I said.

"Nothing else," he murmured, nuzzling my neck. My skin fizzed where his lips touched, and I had to concentrate to rap him on the back of the head.

"Yes," I said. "Nothing else."

He sat back, eyes clouded with lust slowly clearing. "I am what you are, Love: a child of the gods. Well, I am closer than you: my mother was a goddess. Your grandmother is the actual godling in your family."

My heart stalled. Child of the gods? Me? *Nana?*

Actually, I had to admit that made a hell of a lot of sense. Nana's bizarre observations, her uncanny sense of timing, her ridiculous physical abilities... I blinked, unsure what was more unsettling: that my grandmother was a godling, or that it was dead easy to believe it.

"Hold on, wait," I said, wriggling further out from underneath Brandr. "If you're a godling, then..." I hesitated, not sure how to phrase my question, and not sure I wanted to know the answer.

A godling. No wonder girls of all ages threw themselves at him. How many women had he loved in his lifetime? Ten? Twenty? A hundred?

Cold logic was almost as good as a cold shower.

"No," I said. "No."

"No what?"

"No as in I-am-*not*-going-to-be-the-latest-in-a-long-line-of-floozies-no." I shook my head. "Not interested. I don't care what you are, I'm not available."

His eyes widened, body and face alike drooping in disappointment. "But Love, you feel it, I know you do."

"Feel what?" I snapped, arms wrapped tightly around my torso. I felt nothing that he didn't manipulate me to feel with his stupid godly powers.

"This," he whispered, and reached out.

His fingertip connected softly with the corner of my jaw, and I swallowed against the melting heat that tried to consume me.

His finger trailed down my neck, tracing a blissful line across the hollow of my clavicle, lighting fire oh-so-carefully down my sternum.

He pulled away and I remembered how to breathe.

"See?" he said, still whispering. "How can you deny it?"

I shook my head, tears burning my eyes. *I don't want this, I don't want this,* I reminded myself frantically. "It isn't real."

My nails dug into my palms as I stared into his sea-green eyes, so full of sadness they seemed a mirror of my own. "Tell me..." I drew in a shaky breath. "Answer the question."

He nodded, gaze searching my face like an enigma.

"How many other girls?"

Brandr frowned, and sadness turned to confusion.

I rolled my eyes, flicking away tears with a quick finger. "Don't give me that. How many other girls have you played this game with, made... feel like this?"

I wasn't holding my breath for his answer. I wasn't.

His confusion deepened. "But Love, I couldn't."

It was my turn to be confused. "What do you mean?"

He shook his head. "I couldn't *make* someone feel like this. When I touch you, I feel what you feel. I felt it that first time, do you remember? The massage?"

Saints, how I had tried to forget. His touches had been perfectly innocent, utterly professional, but the fire they'd awoken in me had left me reeling in terror; I'd never felt anything so strong in my life.

A tiny smile played at the corners of his mouth. "That's when I knew."

My heart pounded in my head, my chest... "Knew what?"

He was leaning closer, lips a mere breath away, and I didn't want to be a conquest, but now that I thought about it—really and truly thought about it, without the filter of frustration and jealousy—could it be? Was I really the only girl actually losing her head over this man, the only one struggling not to throw herself at his feet?

"I knew," he whispered against my ear, and I almost couldn't hear him through the ecstasy echoing through my body, "that you were the one."

"I don't believe in soulmates," I whispered back, eyes closed, every sense in my body standing to attention as his cheek tickled against mine.

"You don't have to." His lips traced my jaw and I shivered. "Your heart recognises me, Love, whether you believe in it or not."

"Love," I whispered, fingers tightening in his hair. "Is that what this is?"

"Not yet," he said. "But it could be. If you wanted it to be."

I luxuriated in the thought for just a moment, before another one hit me. I bolted upright, narrowly avoiding a collision with his nose. "Wait just one second here, buddy. Old? You think I look tired and old?" His words from that morning rang in my ear. "Not to mention, oh, I don't know, my too-broad shoulders and my totally-lost forehead!" I glared at him, wishing that godling powers included the ability to set someone literally on fire.

Brandr laughed, a soft, throaty chuckle that sounded far too appealing. "I knew you'd take it like that, and I confess, I half hoped I'd provoke you into responding. But if you recall, I said that *some* things around here were getting downright old and worn. I mean, Love, your constant indifference. Not *you*."

He tracked a finger over my hairline, leaving tingling fireworks in its wake.

"That's nice," I said, pushing his hand away, "But what about my shoulders? And my forehead?"

He frowned, confusion plain again. "What about them?"

"You…" I squirmed, uncertain how to voice my fears aloud without sounding insecure and needy. "They're not 'too broad', and, well, you know…?"

"Look at me, Love," he said. "Am I perfect?"

YES, my heart screamed. YES YOU ARE BLOODY PERFECT. But I shoved the scrambling emotions away and forced myself to look.

Cold logic; cold shower; I could do this. And true, now he mentioned it, his nose leaned a bit to one side, and one eye was slightly larger than the other, and if I was going to be utterly picky then his forehead was probably a fraction too large, and… "Oh."

Brandr softened into a smile. "Answer the question, Love."

"Yes," I said. "And no. I see what you mean. You mean that—"

He pressed a finger against my lips. "Answer the question, Love, but nothing else." His eyes sparkled.

I smiled.

He leaned down and kissed me, and this time, I kissed him back.

THE MAKING OF
ANSWER THE QUESTION

This was never actually a story: it was a dream.

I mean that. Like, literally. This whole story was a dream I had one night in its entirety, from the pastel green day spa to the cobalt blue water bottle to the red silk blouse to the glimmering strands of the necklace/headdress/magical jewellery *thing*.

Why on earth else would he have swept her up onto his shoulders and pranced around an expensive boutique store like that?

Clearly I was dreaming.

I'm just impressed that it resulted in a narrative that made sense.

And let's be real: don't we all dream of someone who can make us feel that way?

DOWNLOAD YOUR FREE EBOOK

When you buy a print book from Inkprint Press, we like to say THANK YOU by offering you the ebook for free!

Please head to www.inkprintpress.com/inklets/10/ and the use the coupon 10INKLET to get your copy of this Inklet in epub AND mobi today!
(Coupon will only work once.)

HOW NOT TO ACQUIRE A CASTLE

CHAPTER ONE

ON A HARD PLASTIC CHAIR IN THE FRONT row of the Great Hall in the world's fifth-best evil overlording academy, with its red-wooden parquetry floor that spoke of wealth and the beige, square panels of sound-boards speaking of conservatism on the walls, Mercury sat, pointedly not sweating.

Partly, this was because the Academy Administrators had deigned to turn on the air-conditioning earlier in the day, in recognition of the fact that the hall would be packed out with approximately six hundred bodies, all here to celebrate the graduation of about a third of that crowd.

But mostly, Mercury was pointedly not sweating because she made it a point never to sweat, sweat being an indication that she was working hard, and hard work being antithetical to her way of life.

However. If she *had* been sweating right now, it would not have been due to the uncomfortable warmth of six hundred packed bodies that even the air-conditioning system couldn't completely shift, or, in fact, from overexertion. Instead, it would have been caused by an even more unfamiliar concept in Mercury's emotional vocabulary: nervousness.

Mercury did not *get* nervous. Mercury got things *done*.

So the fact that she was sitting here, in the front row of the Great Hall, about to graduate from Evil Overlording Academy (with distinction), and was feeling *nervous*... She crumpled the black paper program in her pale fists. It made her furious, that's what it did.

Abjectly furious, that snooty-tooty Deviran with his stupid morals and his stupid I-don't-want-to-be-here and his stupid Overlords-are-empty-figureheads and his stupid face sitting ten people over, looking implacable with his deep brown skin and barely-there, precision-groomed beard, as though he knew it gave him a stupid air of alluringly stupid mystery…

Mercury scowled and searched for the train of thought that had been derailed, yet again, by Deviran's stupidity.

Ah. Yes. She was angry because she was nervous because she wasn't absolutely entirely one hundred and fifty percent sure that she'd beaten Deviran in their final exams, and 1) being anything less than a hundred and fifty percent certain of anything made her cranky, and 2) being beaten by Deviran for dux of the year would be utterly unbearable. She flicked away a piece of fluff that had become snagged under her immaculately magenta-painted nails and smoothed out the black paper program.

In the front corner of the hall, the starkly-attired string quartet with their traditional black instruments began playing the March of the Oncoming Doom. The screechy scrapes of hundreds of chairs on the hall's wooden floor sounded as the crowd climbed to its collective feet.

Mercury sat with her arms firmly folded for a few moments longer, until her best friend Sparky kicked her in the ankle.

"Get up, idiot," Sparky hissed, hints of real flame flickering through her flame-coloured pixie cut.

"No," Mercury said, flouncing to her feet and tossing her own glossy brown hair back over her shoulders. Four years she'd been playing by the Academy's rules in order to get what she wanted, and she'd had just about enough. Other people's rules should only be applied to plebs too stupid to invent their own.

Sparky rolled her eyes somewhere over Mercury's head before focusing on the stage, where the ceremonial party had begun entering.

Mercury clenched her jaw and narrowed her own eyes as the teachers of the Evil Overlording Academy filed onto the stage, dressed in their formal finery. Each teacher had their own distinctive look that matched their personality and their Overlording style, from severe charcoal suits to jet-black leathers, pastel ball-gowns and gem-toned lingerie and eye-blinding spandex, and even on one tiny old woman at the back, worn jeans and a grey flannel shirt. She was the one to watch out for, of course; Mercury could respect an Overlord who was confident enough in their abilities that they didn't need to telegraph them. It wasn't a look *she* would consider, of course, but still. She could respect it.

The band's march finished and, after a moderately awkward pause, the crowd sat. The Principal, pale skin and dark hair matching his suspiciously vampiric red-and-black suit, took the podium, and Mercury narrowed her eyes. He was doing a superb job of hiding his emotions—he was a premier Evil Overlord, after all—but she was Mercury, and unlike anyone else, she had the benefit of being able to rummage through people's consciousnesses. She was better at adding things *into* people's minds than taking information out, but he was telegraphing fear loudly enough that she could sense it without trying overly much.

Mercury pursed her lips.

Hmm.

The Principal cleared his throat at the blackened-wood podium, and the fear made it into his usually-unreadable eyes. "Before we begin," he said, and Mercury's stomach did a peculiar kind of flip-flop. "I have a pressing announcement to make regarding the safety of our students and their families."

He cleared his throat again and took out a sheet of paper from his pocket, unfolding it carefully and smooth-ing out the creases before beginning again. "The Council"—quiet booing echoed around the hall, and Mercury tsked impatiently— "have asked me to recommend that stu-dents from Tumul Tuos seriously consider postponing their return to town for a few days. The city is dealing with a *situation* at present which may present a danger to our students' health and safety."

Mercury's hands fisted at her sides and she forced herself to remain seated. What was wrong with her city? What had the Council mucked up now? A risk to the students' safety? There had to be more he wasn't telling them. Gently, Mercury tugged on his consciousness, implanting the suggestion that it might be better to share the news than to keep it secret. After all, how could they fight an enemy they didn't know?

"There are, ah..." He trailed off, glancing side to side as though wondering why his mouth had decided to continue.

Mercury didn't snicker, but she did press her lips together in satisfaction.

The Principal took a deep, steadying breath and seemed to change tack. "There has been one death already. The family have already been notified, so it is with much regret that I must inform you that Woovermyer will no longer be with us at the Evil Overlording Academy."

Murmurs broke out around the room, not all of them sad—to be expected in a school devoted to raising the next generation of dictators (ish) and despots (of sorts).

Mercury, however, crushed her program in her left hand, fist so tight her nails bit her palm.

"You okay?" Sparky murmured, leaning towards her.

Mercury gave a single, tense shake of her head and stared at the podium. Dead. Livie Woovermyer was dead in *her city*. And the Council hadn't done anything to stop it. Couldn't do anything to stop it, probably, given they'd warned the students to stay away. Livie hadn't been the strongest candidate in the year level, but she was no lightweight, either. It would take a lot of power to kill a Seven.

Enough was enough. A good thing Mercury was about to graduate at the top of the class, giving her the right to knock the lowest ranking current Overlord off their perch. Tumul Tuos would be hers in a matter of hours. And then there'd be no more of these wasteful deaths. Her city would be safe at last.

Madame Pompadour was up the front now, elbow gloves the same glimmery silver colour as her elaborate, piled-curls wig, eyelids gleaming with matching silver eye shadow, and abruptly Mercury realised Madame was there to make the announcement that would change her life forever. She leaned forward in her seat, ready to stand when her name was called.

"And now the announcement you've all been dying for," the Political Alliances teacher trilled, the frills on her evening gown fluttering as she moved. "The dux of this year's cohort!"

Sweat slicked Mercury's palms. Irritated, she reached over and wiped them on Sparky's thigh.

Sparky pushed Mercury's hands back into her own personal space bubble and Mercury, nervous to the edge of distraction, let her.

"Will you please join me in welcoming to the stage, our wonderful dux for this year, Deviran Goodsmith!"

Mercury froze halfway to standing. "Did she just say Deviran?" she whispered furiously to Sparky.

Sparky hauled her forcibly back down into her seat. "Yes," she hissed back. "Sit down, you're making a fool of yourself."

Mercury's spine snapped upright as she sat, and she arranged the folds of her long black skirt demurely. "No I'm not." She closed her eyes. "Deviran's going up to the stage, isn't he?" Even at a whisper, the misery in her voice was clear, but this time, she didn't care.

Sparky reached over and squeezed her hand.

Mercury squeezed back, lacing her fingers through Sparky's, and held tight as all her plans and dreams vanished in front of her.

A stone had landed in her chest. That must be it. Some strange sort of magic that made her chest contract and sink, and made the world distort for just a moment, long enough to trick her into thinking Deviran had beaten her so that someone could jump in front of her and yell SURPRISE!

Any moment now.

Any moment.

She refused to open her eyes and watch Deviran parading across the stupid stage like some stupid stupid-person, receiving his stupid medal and stupid symbolic crest pin.

It was that last exam question. She'd known Deviran would pull out his ridiculous 'Evil Overlords are merely figureheads, the Business Guild is where the power really lies' rant that everyone had heard a million times back when he was younger and angrier, and she'd tried to counter it, she really had.

She'd argued for the importance of the Overlording position, for the power of having a symbolic figure to unite the population in their hatred, for having a person able to make all the difficult, necessary decisions the Council was too weak and spineless to make... But it hadn't been enough. Everything she'd worked for, everything she'd set out to prove—and it wasn't enough.

There were words, there were names, and then forever later, once she'd died twice already, Sparky elbowed her in the ribs. "Come on," Sparky muttered. "We're up next."

And sure enough, there was a shuffling of presenters as the last of the Powers Behind The Thone graduates departed the stage, and the next speaker announced in threatening, funereal tones, "The Overlording cohort."

Mercury blinked furiously and followed Sparky to the end of the line at the right side of the stage. The other candidates proceeded one at a time across the stage, two girls and then stupid Deviran, and then a handful more and then Sparky, and then the speaker was calling her name.

Hands fisted, Mercury tossed her head high, climbed the four steps, and marched across the stage. She wouldn't look at them, the stupid faculty who'd denied her the city she rightfully deserved, and she wouldn't look the other way either, at the classmates and crowd undoubtedly sniggering at her failure.

She shook hands with the presenter, and while he pinned the tiny crossed-swords badge on her collar, her eyes betrayed her and slid towards the audience. Her stomach flipped as she saw the crowd of parents and friends behind the rows of students, all the way to the back of the hall, twenty rows at least, illuminated by the late afternoon light streaming in through the ceiling-high windows to the right. Everyone had someone here to watch them graduate. Everyone except Weird Al—and her.

The presenter finished with her pin, muttered something to her, and offered his hand again. Mercury coldly ignored it and strode from the stage. It didn't matter. None of it mattered. Tumul Tuos was her city anyway, and no one could change that. She'd think of something. She'd take a day or two out, make some plans…

And she could always hope that Deviran would choose some other Overlording territory. He'd be stupid to, but then again, he was stupid, so. Mercury could hope.

All at once, mid-way down the steps off the stage, Mercury came to rigid attention, scanning the room. Somewhere out there in the crowd, an exchange of power had just taken place, and it felt… unusual.

But the final few students were backing up behind her and muttering, so Mercury headed back toward her seat, craning her head all the while and searching for some sign of whatever it was that had just discharged a dizzyingly quiet amount of power into the room.

She sat, and Sparky leaned over. "Okay?"

"Mm," said Mercury. "Did you feel…" She accidentally caught the eye of the student behind her and twisted back to face the front.

"Feel what?"

Mercury turned it over in her mind. It had felt like a large shot of power discharged very quietly—but perhaps it hadn't been. Perhaps it had only been a small discharge after all, something most people wouldn't have noticed.

But still, something about it had tugged on her. It very nearly felt like something she'd felt before, only she *knew* she'd never sensed that kind of discharge before.

She shook her head. "Never mind. Don't worry."

Sparky sighed and straightened. "It's fine, Mercury," she said, drily exasperated.

"I know you didn't win, but I promise, you'll live through it."

Mercury waved a hand for silence.

The power had just discharged again, and it had come from somewhere in the back corner, far away from the windows and light.

Impatiently, Mercury waited for the formalities to conclude. The crowd stood while the quartet played the exit march, and the stage party left, Mercury tapping her foot all the while.

The moment the last notes of the march died away, Mercury turned and headed to the back corner, weaving in and out of the students and parents who had seemed to explode slowly but inexorably out from the neat rows of seating, ignoring Sparky's calls behind her. Power, something that tugged in a way that was strange and familiar, all at once. She pushed her way through a family posing for pictures—and halted.

In the shadows of the back corner, Deviran stood with his family, with his stupid, smug little smile, looking as tall and dark and stupidly alluring as ever. Prat.

His mother, short but sleek, and his father—tall, and utterly terrifying in a way not at all diminished by his gleaming smile—gushed over him, patting his back and hugging him tight. Within moments the Principal was there, glibly shaking hands and congratulating them on the success of their son. Something flickered across his consciousness, and also Deviran's father's—some moment of recognition in response to what they were saying.

But Mercury brushed it aside just as the mother brushed melodramatic tears from her cheeks and handed Deviran a silver-wrapped package about as long as her hand but half the width.

That. That was the source of the strange, magical feeling. Mercury watched hawk-eyed as Deviran un-wrapped the gift. A glimpse of gold set her pulse racing—What was it? What did it do? Could she steal it?—and then the paper fell away to the floor, and Deviran stood staring wordlessly at the object in his hands, and Mercury did too.

Wide-eyed, Deviran raised his gaze to his parents, and even from where she stood Mercury could hear the reverence in his voice as he thanked them.

But Mercury had eyes only for the object. No wonder she'd felt it discharge, and no wonder it had felt both strange and familiar. In Deviran's hands lay a glorious, sunshine-gold key, large and strong—and with a handle in the shape of a stylised fish, long, flowing fins curving to make the grip.

A Key. They'd given him a Key. And not just any Key, but *the* Key, *her* Key, the Artefact of Power belonging to *her* city.

A wordless noise of wanting rose in Mercury's throat. Who cared about being dux? She needed that Key.

Keep reading! Head to
http://www.amylaurens.com/
books/kaditeos/castle
to buy your copy now!

ABOUT THE AUTHOR

AMY LAURENS is an Australian author of fantasy fiction for all ages—and somehow, the romance just keeps creeping in too. One day, she'll write a real-world romance without magic, just to prove that she can.

On the other hand, isn't romance a kind of magic of its own?

Amy certainly thinks so: she's happily married to her own perfect romance hero, and together they have two children who keep them busy, and are definitely not fodder for Amy's social media feeds.

You can find out more about Amy at her website, www.amylaurens.com.

INKLETS

Collect them all! Released on the 1st and 15th of each month.

INKLET #007
SEVENTY
LIANA BROOKS

INKLET #008
A Final Request for Mercy
AMY LAURENS

INKLET #009
the kitten psychologist
vs.
the kitten's owners
THEA VAN DIEPEN

INKLET #010
Answer the Question
AMY LAURENS

INKLET #011
Happily, Red
AMY LAURENS

INKLET #012
the kitten psychologist
tries to be patient
through email
THEA VAN DIEPEN

INKLET #013
DRAGON Tuesday
AMY LAURENS

INKLET #014
RED PLANET REFUGEES
LIANA BROOKS

INKLET #015
the kitten psychologist &
What The Kitten Did
THEA VAN DIEPEN

Cherry
Blossom
AMY LAURENS

Alone
AMY LAURENS

the kitten psychologist
& The Kitten
Come To A Conclusion
THEA VAN DIEPEN

LEVEL NINE
LIANA BROOKS

To Dust
AMY LAURENS

Interchange
AMY LAURENS

Emalia's
Lanterns
LIANA BROOKS

Dear Santa
AMY LAURENS

The
Quilt-Maker's
Scrap
AMY LAURENS